Ghosts
of
Pennsylvania's Susquehanna River

© Bruce Carlson 2010

All rights reserved. No part of this book may be reproduced or transmitted in any form or by any means, electronic or mechanical, including photocopying, recording or by any informational storage or retrieval system, except by a reviewer who may quote brief passages in a review to be printed in a magazine or newspaper without permission in writing from the publisher.

Table of Contents

Watching You 13
The Nose Knows 25
Come On Over 29
Ghosts Of Clay 41
The Corpse 51
The Big Squeeze 57
The Hand 61
Gold From The River 65
A Bubble Off 69
Paintin' The Coop 83
The Flower Girl 89
The Tap On The Shoulder 95
Down The Stairs 103
The Odd Case Of Dimples Darmhoff 107
The Inconvenience 117

The reader should understand that we were able to obtain some of these stories only if we promised to obscure some of the actual identity of persons and/or property. This required us to occasionally use fictitious names. In such cases, the names of the people and/or the places are not to be confused with actual places or actual persons living or dead.

As one drives along the Susquehanna River, there is little to suggest it has its mysteries. As it flows through Pennsylvania's countryside, there is little that hints of its secrets.

But those waters, and their shores, do hold stories of things unseen and unexplained things. This book is about some of those unexplained things. It's about some of those mysteries of our Susquehanna.

Watching You

Back in the '20s and '30s, Roy and Liz Sinke lived in a really nice home overlooking the Susquehanna River, just out of Harrisburg.

The Sinke home was pretty much the social hub of the area, and an invitation to that house was prized by friends and acquaintances.

Roy Sinke had two main passions in life, one being hunting and the other that of playing host to guests in their home.

And one of the few things that allowed Roy to combine those two passions was a little practical joke he would play on houseguests. This consisted of his manipulating a little control device in his pocket, hidden away there so he could work that mechanism without being detected. He could stand there visiting with a guest about one thing or the other, and with one hand casually in his pocket running that little assemblage of wires and levers and buttons, all at the same time.

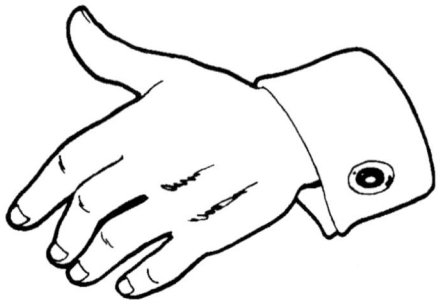

For those times back in the '20s and '30s, that little control mechanism was at the cutting edge of technology. It was connected, via radio waves, to a small receptor hidden within the hair on the neck of one of two trophies hanging there on the wall of their great room. That little receptor would, in turn, direct some tiny motors within the trophies to kick in or out as Roy would dictate from where he would be so innocently standing chatting with a guest about this or that.

While there were a number of trophies up on the walls of that great room, only two of them were wired up so they would move.

The movement that the system was capable of was only that of the head moving up or down or back or forth. But, that was enough to accomplish what Roy wanted. He wanted one or the other of those trophies to "follow," with its eyes, a specific person there in the room.

By manipulating that control device he had in his pocket. Roy could cause one of those stuffed animals up there on the wall to follow the movements of that nice lady from York, or one of his business associates, or whoever he chose.

No matter where in the room his victim would go, the critter up there on the wall would follow him or her with its eyes, following the person relentlessly.

The two that were wired up to make that happen was a large buck deer over by one of the doorways and the other was a huge gray wolf. That wolf was in the process of climbing a rock "cliff," staring down into the room. That "cliff" was actually part of the decorative stonework built around the fireplace. The fireplace, the stone cliff and that gray wolf dominated the east wall of the room, and served as a striking focal point for the entire room.

The wolf had a very solemn look on his face, and had blue-gray eyes that would seem to look into a person, boring into him until it felt like the thing was looking at your very soul. Just to look at that thing head on was kind of a spooky experience, but if you suddenly realized that the wolf was "following" you with those eyes as you wandered around the room, it would bring "wandering" to a total halt. Many, when realizing what was going on, would flee the room and come back in only with reluctance. The whole arrangement, especially that wolf scene, cost Roy a really nice piece of change, but it gave him so much fun that he considered it to be well worth it.

The buck deer was spooky enough in its own right, but the wolf was something else.

Martha, Roy's wife, was fully aware of the reality of that wolf's "watching" people, but even she would get real spooked by that thing, and forbade her husband turning that wolf loose on her.

What Roy would do would be to pick out one of his guests, always one who had not been to his house before, and make that particular individual the butt of his joke.

Roy would simply manipulate that control mechanism in his pocket to cause one of those trophies to continually watch his victim. If the person in the hot seat was the new neighbor's wife, no matter where in the room she went, the head and eyes of one of those trophies would be following her.

This was a particularly effective joke to play when he'd use the wolf. The solemn look on the wolf's face made the thing look all the more weird, more spooky than if the face had shown a snarl or viciousness of some other kind.

When the victim of Roy's joke would discover that he was being watched by one of those animals, it would make him quickly forget his mission of finding some more stuffed olives or miniature pickles over there on the hors d'oeuvres table.

Both the hors d'oeuvres table and the table set up for drinks would always be placed over by the wall. Mrs. Sinke learned that guests, suspecting something odd about one or the other of those trophies, would be watching that thing so intently that he'd walk right into those two little tables.

All in all, it was a fun little thing of Roy to pull on his guests on occasion. He didn't do it every time he had guests. Even the question of if he would or not would add an element of suspense to any event there at the Sinke house.

The Sinkes were rather well to do people and could afford frequent entertaining and afford the costs of clever little things like those two trophies.

There was an unwritten, but firm, rule that houseguests who knew about these trophies were not to tell others about it.
Roy needed a fresh victim each time and didn't want to be pulling his laborious little trick on someone who already knew about it.

That unwritten rule didn't have to be written down. Invitations to the Sinke home were so valued that no one would spill the beans and risk not getting invited to those gala events anymore.

Sometimes the situation would be revealed to the victim that no matter where he went in the room, one of those critters would be watching him. Sometimes a fellow guest would "notice" what was going on and point out to the victim that he was constantly being watched by the critter up there on the wall. It was when this would happen that the furniture would get stumbled over as the victim would check the trophy to see if that was really true. When you are striding purposefully from one end of the room and discovering that one of those critters was watching your every move, it was easy to find yourself knocking over furniture or other guests.

The most fun for Roy and others in the room would happen when the guest would discover, for himself, that he was being watched. A sudden flash in the room from Roy's camera would alert those in the room that Roy had gotten a photo of one really shocked guest when he or she would discover what was going on.

A woman, discovering that she was being watched, would invariably scream and flee the room. The men who were victimized by their host would step back a couple steps, especially when the "watcher" was that wolf.

While being the butt of Roy's little joke was always an unnerving experience, the victim would at least know that he or she had achieved the ultimate social standing in the community as a result of what they had to go through.

On occasion, Roy would let one of his guests run the mechanism, thus playing the trick on another one of them.

The Sinkes lived in that house for many years, enjoying the fruits of Roy's business plus an inheritance that Martha had received.

Roy passed away in 1937, putting an end to his fun and games.

On occasion, a guest would ask Martha if he could play Roy's old trick at dinner parties and other doings at the home. Martha would almost always concur, so Roy's little trick survived him by a number of years.

Those events at the home involving only ladies, such as teas, charity committee meetings, and so forth, were never occasions where either the deer or the wolf would kick in. That trick was sort of a macho kind of thing, one that would always involve memories of Roy.

Often, when the trophy trick would get played after Roy's death, Martha would be seen with a smile on her face, enjoying the joke as much as anyone else, but also with a tear in her eye as she would recall those golden years with Roy.

Prior to Martha's death in 1949, she was playing hostess to a dinner party there at the house. By this time, she was getting up in years and the festivities at the Sinke home had become considerably quieter than they had been in the old days. But, invitations to the Sinke home were still coveted by many.

By this time, there were as many social events at the home that didn't involve the trophies as there were those that did.

Martha didn't engage in that herself, and that old "watching" trick got played only when a guest would ask to be able to manipulate those controls.

It was at a dinner party in 1949 when a grinning guest came out into the hallway to tell Martha that one of the other guests was assuredly playing Roy's old trick on one of the other guests.

Martha smiled and allowed as to how it was nice that the guests were enjoying themselves.

"And, that wolf always gave that old trick of Roy's a special kick since it was such a sinister looking animal."

"Oh, no, Martha, whoever is running those controls in there is using the deer head over the doorway. You should come in and join in on the fun."

That guest wouldn't have had to suggest that. Martha was scurrying into the Great Room as fast as her elderly feet could carry her.

As Martha entered the room, she could tell that the victim of the joke had just discovered he was being watched, and was gasping in shock over how that deer head was watching him.

As Martha entered the room, a lot of the guests watched her. She was a Grande Dame now, loved by many and admired by all.

What they saw wasn't that always self-composed Martha Sinke. She came into the room with a look of dismay and disbelief in her eyes. She immediately sought out that deer head, and saw, as had the others, that it was moving.

Those looks of concern changed to looks of shock as Martha fainted dead away, right there onto the floor.

After a number of "back offs" and "give her airs," Martha came around again, again with a look of dismay and shock on her face.

The perpetrator of the little trick was at Martha's side, feeling guilty about his somehow causing his hostess to react so much to his trick.

A friend rushed to Martha's side. Martha came around and looked back and forth between her friend and the deer head on the wall.

"That deer head isn't the one Roy had up there all those years. That one got to losing some hunks of hair, so I had the groundskeeper haul that to the basement and bring up this other one. This one isn't wired up to do Roy's trick."

Thinking that Martha might well not be rational for some reason, a neighbor enlisted the aid of another of the men guests, went next door to his garage and carried a ladder over to the house, bringing it into the great room. He meant to inspect the deer head, then be able to assure Martha that she must be misremembering the situation. He wanted to assure his hostess that everything was quite normal, and that she should probably retire to take a nap.

The neighbor, there on the ladder, found a surprise. That deer head up there, was indeed a different one. This fellow had been privy to how that little mechanism up there was hidden in the hair of the trophy, but this one had no such accessory.

When he made that announcement, the room turned real quiet as the people sought to understand what was happening. Those guests who had watched the trophy "following" the victim as he walked around the room were now looking at that thing in a different way.

How could that have happened if this was just another deer head, not the one Roy had wired up for his trick?

It was obvious from that day on that Roy Sinke had come back to play his trick one more time, enjoying his playing host there in that old home overlooking the Susquehanna.

Apparently as a ghost, Roy didn't need all the little wires and buttons to make it all happen.

The Nose Knows

There must be a reason why ghosts generally make themselves known to us only through three of our senses…our senses of sound, sight and feel.

The writer has no more of an idea of why that is than anyone else, but it does seem to be true.

If there's one ghost who has announced his presence by showing up at the foot of a bed, there have been a thousand of them that used our sense of sight to let us know they are there.

And, if there has been one that has made his presence known by slamming doors or clanking chains, there have been a thousand of those also.

And of course, now and then, our spiritual friends will put in an appearance by one feeling something like cold air or something..…or maybe the feel of someone sitting on the edge of the bed when one is laying in it.

That's how most of 'em do it……….by letting us know about them through our senses of sound, sight or feel.

The ghosts in the Wilson home in Selinsgrove had another way, another means of making their presence known. Their way was through our sense of smell.

Well, it wasn't really the Wilson home. All they did was buy the place with their hard-earned money. All they did was do all the work, buy the insurance, pay the taxes and keep the place fixed up.

That's all they did. So the place certainly should have been known in the Selinsgrove area as the Wilson home.

But it wasn't. Everybody called it the Panella place. The Panella family hadn't turned a hand to keep the place up for decades, but it was still known as the Panella place.

Not only did the Wilsons have a put up with that injustice of the place being called the Panella place, but they also had to put up with the Panellas.

Apparently, both Mr. and Mrs. Panella had found it hard to leave the old family place after they died in the 1950s, he in 1952 and she in 1954.

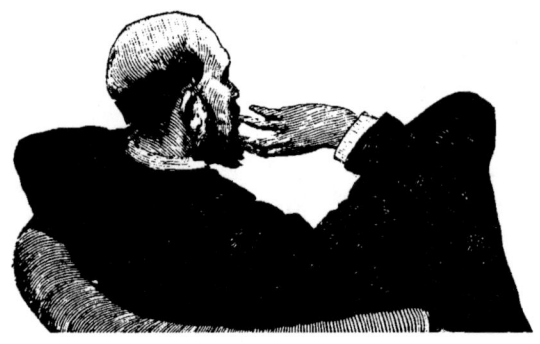

When the Wilsons moved in in 1982 they should have had every reason to think the Panellas were behind them.

After the home had been entirely remodeled and repainted, the Wilsons should have been able to look forward to being shed of the Panellas, but couldn't.

The first sign that that Italian family was still around was the unmistakable aroma of garlic one suppertime. Varna Wilson probably hadn't used garlic even once in her life in cooking, so that smell of garlic certainly wasn't her doing.

But, there was that undeniable odor of garlic.

The odor of garlic isn't something you can dismiss, of course. When you've got that garlic odor in the house, you've got that garlic odor, for sure.

That first episode of the aroma of garlic didn't get explained away as being the work of a ghost at first. It was simply one of those unexplained things.

Then, the next thing that happened was almost worse. There was the odor of homemade wine in the house that was strong enough to peel wallpaper.

The Wilsons had learned from a neighbor that that Old Man Panella had been in the practice of making homemade wine. That was what led the family to think that perhaps the Panellas had returned.

It was then that it occurred to them that ghosts might well be an explanation for that garlic odor earlier.

From then on, it was one Italian odor after the other. If it wasn't the old man's wine working, it was Maria's garlic or oregano.

The Wilsons never did catch sight of their Italian guests, and never heard them clanking chains or stomping around darkened hallways. It was always smells, always strange and always strong. Fortunately those odors were also always temporary.

Odors aren't something you can turn off like a light or a faucet. Odors tend to linger long after the source is gone. But it wasn't that way with the odors that the Wilsons would pick up on there in their house. There could be that wallpaper-peeling odor of homemade wine, and in an instant it would be gone.

This went on for a number of years, then……..just like that, it stopped. Maybe Lormago and Maria got weary of doing their things in the Wilson home.

Come On Over

Greg Hauser and Linus Baxter were neighbors and buddies near Danville. Those two were closer than most brothers. Both were ten years old and vitally interested in swimming, baseball and fishing.

It was an odd day when those boys weren't either engaged in one of those pursuits or, at least, talking about one or the other.

While there was one house between those of the Hauser family and the Baxters, that didn't slow those boys down any. That resourceful pair rigged up an endless loop of clothesline up there hooked onto each of their houses. The line passed through two pulleys so they could send messages back and forth, just by pulling on the loop. Hooked onto the clothesline was a little box. It was into that box they boys would stash their messages to each other.

The boys got the idea for their "telegraph" as they called it, from clotheslines of that design that some of the ladies in the community had. Those clotheslines would string out from the house to a tree or something like that. The boys simply ran it from the windowsill of one house to the windowsill of the other.

That system was great for sending messages back and forth………always secret messages and often in code. They had learned how to write in code from one of the issues of Captain Marvel comics.

Both of the pulleys in that "telegraph" needed a good shot of oil, both of them being pretty rusty.

But, they never got that. Those rusty old pulleys screeched and squeaked away as those secret messages got sent back and forth between those houses. Not only messages would be sent back and forth, but other goodies like cookies, hunks of candy stolen from an unsuspecting sister, or the latest issue of Captain Marvel.

The protests of those overworked and under-greased pulleys could be heard throughout the neighborhood. Whenever anyone heard those pulleys squeaking and growing, they knew those two boys were trading something or other with their "telegraph."

The boys were proud of their system for trading information or goodies back and forth. It was the next best thing to being able to play together.

The boys were given the opportunity to "talk" back and forth for a few exchanges at bedtime.

The bedtime correspondences would eventually have to be stopped by one or the other of the moms. When that happened, the boys knew the day was over and it was time for bed. All they could do then was dream about the foot long bluegills or the homeruns in store for them the next day.

Things went great for the boys in the summer of their tenth year. They had it made, except for what was due to happen on that last week of summer.

It was during that last week of the summer that the Baxters were due to take a weeklong vacation trip.

The boys lobbied hard for the vacation plans to include Greg going with the Baxter family on that trip. But, all that was to no avail. Mrs. Baxter thought the boys needed to be apart for a few days, and Mrs. Hauser agreed.

And so it was. That day came when Linus was to leave for that vacation and Greg couldn't tag along.

It was kind of a bummer sort of day for those two, but they enjoyed a frenzy of swimming and fishing the previous day, so they got that in, at least.

It was on a Friday when the Baxters pulled out of their driveway for what was going to be quite a distance to drive.

Fate was about to deal a severe blow to both families. The days of swimming, fishing and baseball together were over for those two boys.

The Baxter family drove the remainder of that day, plus most of the next to get to their destination. It was toward the end of the trip on that Saturday late afternoon when it happened. The family's station wagon missed a turn in the unfamiliar rough and hilly country they were going through. It plunged down a steep hill and ended up crashing into a large boulder near the base of the hill.

Both Linus and his mother were killed and Mr. Baxter suffered some serious injuries.

By six o'clock that Saturday evening, Mr. Baxter was lying in a hospital bed, and both Linus and his mother were lying in a morgue.

Meanwhile, Greg was totally unaware of the tragedy that had befallen his friend and the rest of the family. He fell in with some other kids around, but his heart wasn't in it. He knew that another Friday would have to roll around before Linus would return.

Greg just figured he'd have to get along doing whatever he could to pass the time. He knew he had to do that for almost a whole week yet.

By Monday morning, word still hadn't gotten back to Danville that the Baxters had been in a car wreck and that Mrs. Baxter and her son were both fatalities.

It was on that Monday morning that Greg had gone to his room upstairs, for lack of anything better to do. He was trying to amuse himself by working on a half-finished model airplane he was building.

Suddenly, Greg heard that familiar old squeak and squeal of the "telegraph." That contraption was working, probably bringing him a message from his buddy.

He was glad to know that, for some reason, the Baxters had come home early from their vacation and he and Linus could get back to the important stuff like fishing and swimming.

Eagerly Greg leaped up from his desk to open the window to get the message.

Upon opening his window and sticking his head out so he could see the length of the "telegraph," he saw the little wooden box lurching its way from Linus' house to his own.

As he waited there for the box to work its way to him, he almost giggled to himself in anticipation of what the message would be. He had the secret decoder page from the Captain Marvel comic right there, hoping Linus would have the message in code.

Within a couple of minutes, Greg was fumbling with the lid on that box, eager to see the note inside.

The note, unfortunately not in code, simply said…….. "Come on over……..Hurry!"

Greg didn't need to be told that twice. His buddy was home and was ready to play.

Greg hurriedly snapped the lid back on the box after scribbling on it…….."Roger." He knew that Linus would wheel the "telegraph" back for his response. He was on his way and wasn't going to tarry.

He grabbed his baseball mitt and took the banister down to the ground floor rather than waste time taking the stairs themselves.

Meanwhile, a totally different drama was playing out near the top of the steep hill behind the Hauser house. A semi truck was giving its driver some serious problems. The brakes gave out and the man found himself going too fast to shift down to a lower gear to get the things stopped, or even slowed down.

About the time Greg was bolting from his room, that problem up on the hill behind their house turned serious………it became a runaway truck situation.

Not being able to do anything else, the truck driver simply leaned on his horn to alert others that he was out of control.

The poor man's problem compounded as he neared the base of that hill with his speed picking up considerably.

We don't know, of course, what all went through the man's head as he realized that in a few seconds, he'd be airborne as the truck would certainly not be able to make that curve just shy of the first house in the little collection of houses below him.

It was in that second, during which the big old truck was airborne, that Greg was slamming the door shut, getting ready to run across the yard and out across the neighbor's yard to get to Linus' house.

Greg had gotten only three or four strides across the yard when he was knocked to the ground by a flying clothes hamper. That clothes hamper, as well as other things, went flying as that truck crashed down through the roof of the Hauser home. The truck plowed into the upstairs bedroom, wiped out the stairwell, and then destroyed that entire end of the house.

Fully half of the house was little more than kindling within a matter of seconds.

That clothes hamper that caught up with Greg out in the yard was the hamper that occupied his bedroom, the bedroom that no longer existed.

Greg didn't realize yet, as he struggled to regain his footing, that his room was gone or that pieces of it were still raining down into the yard around him.

Finally getting his footing again. Greg turned around to see what had hit him. It was then that he realized that half of their house was gone.

Even as Greg stood there in a daze trying to fathom what had happened, neighbors came rushing over to see what had happened and to see what they could do to help.

Shortly, the police arrived.

It took a few minutes for the police to locate the rest of the family. Greg's father had gone to work and his mother had gone down to the bank on an errand.

The couple got together and rushed home to find their house destroyed, a semi upside down in the living room and their confused son in the capable hands of a helpful neighbor.

In all the excitement, no heed was made to the now tangled up cord and pulleys that had been the boys' telegraph.

By Monday afternoon, the police came up with a surprising message. They had been advised that two days previously the Baxter family had been in an accident several hundred miles away and that both Mrs. Baxter and their son had lost their lives in that accident.

Upon hearing that news, Greg told his parents that that could not be true because he had just that day gotten a message on their "telegraph" from Linus.

37

In fact, the young man told the police that they got their information wrong. He told them of how he had gotten a message just that day and was on his way to Linus' place to play, what with Linus getting back early and all.

Conflicting information as to the fate of three of the citizens led the police to search for the message that Greg claimed to have gotten.

Amid the tangle of pieces of the house, strewn around furniture and broken off tree limbs, the officer found the little wood box.

Mr. and Mrs. Hauser then figured out why Greg had taken the news of the loss of the Baxters so calmly. He had been calm because he knew the reports of the death of Linus were wrong.

This new development provided the police, the neighbors and the Hausers a lot of comfort.

That is, it provided them with comfort until it was established by the authorities in both towns when they talked by phone and the bad news was confirmed.

The entire Hauser incident was very thoroughly investigated, given the conflicting information.

While the police could not put it in their reports that the ghost of young Linus Baxter had delivered a message to Greg in order to get him out of the house, it was generally agreed by all that was, indeed, what had happened.

Greg Hauser had been able to cheat certain death by just a few seconds. It was those few seconds that his fishin' buddy had provided him.

Boys still undoubtedly build telegraphs and other things for their enjoyment. There will be few of them who lose their lives, then go on to save the life of a buddy using those playtime objects.

Ghosts Of Clay

Janice Goodman shared with the author of this book a story that spanned a good portion of her life.

It all started out when Janice was a young girl, living on a farm south of Sayre, along the Susquehanna River.

"I recall my childhood now and am a bit embarrassed at how superficial and shallow I was back then."

"Why do you say that?" I asked.

Janice went on to tell me about her childhood there on the farm. She quickly focused in on her relationship, or lack of relationship, with the neighbors down the road just one farm.

She told me of how neither she nor anyone else in her family had anything to do with the neighbors since they were "odd."

'I know, now, that they were odd in a way that it would be wonderful if we were all so odd."

Apparently this family was pretty much avoided by other families in the neighborhood, also.

Janice told of how she knew very little about the family, but one thing she did know was that the members of the family would fashion figures out of clay there on the farm. They would laboriously create little people, farm animals, little buildings, etc. and paint them up, adding clothes to the figures of people, tiny dog collars to the images of the dogs and make tiny, tiny little harnesses for the horses.

She had seen a few of these that the children in that Leaman family would bring to school for some sort of show and tell thing.

Janice and the other classmates would scoff at these representations of life on the Leaman farm, since such a thing wasn't at all "cool" to the rest of the kids.

Janice told of how she had seen the children of that family flee the front of the room, mortified at the teasing and laughter of the other children.

"I was just shallow enough and cruel enough that I joined in with my classmates in our making fun of those Leaman children. I would give anything, now, if I could have those days back to be a decent person rather than what I was."

I could see that whatever ghostly elements there were going to be about this story, it was also going to be a self-cleansing process for Janice Goodman.

Janice continued on with her story. The story tells of how she grew into high school and then off to college. As in the elementary years of school, Janice had avoided the Leaman family in high school. And, when she was off to college, she pretty much put that family behind her. She had lots of other interests to occupy her thoughts.

Janice came home to Sayre after college and married a local boy from there.

Janice and Harold lived in a house in town for several years, returning to her old neighborhood only for visits to her parents.

Everything was pretty much the same in the old neighborhood as it had been since her childhood, including the Leaman family still living on the farm next door.

While Janice had matured a lot since her childhood, she still had little to do with the Leamans, now out of habit more than out of thoughtlessness.

When Mr. Leaman died, his widow and one or two remaining children moved off the place, and it ended up for sale.

The sale went badly for the Leamans, yielding next to nothing for their possessions. Janice's husband, Harold, had attended the sale. He quickly made a phone call to Janice when the land was being bid on. It was apparent the land was going to go really, really cheaply, and he and Janice had talked of buying a little place in the country and building a new house.

Janice was familiar with the place and told her husband that he should go ahead and bid as he saw fit.

That's what he did, finding it necessary to bid considerably less than he had thought it was worth.

He got it, and suddenly Janice found herself with the prospect of moving into an old house next door to her parents. They knew they'd have to spend a year or two in that old house before tearing it down to make room for a new one.

All this was pretty exciting, of course, and events transpired rapidly, too rapidly for Janice to think much of how that nearby place she had so callously avoided all those years was going to end up her own homestead.

That old house, like all old ones, had to be dusted out pretty well, and some of the residue of the Leamans tossed out. There was stuff in the garage, some in the basement and some in the attic.

Janice and Harold spent one entire weekend doing just that, dragging stuff out of here and there and pitching in the pickup to haul away.

There was little that was salvageable from those tucked away corners of the place. They found a few yard tools, a car jack and a box up in the attic that was carefully wrapped up, apparently overlooked by the Leamans when they left.

It was that box that brings us this story. The box proved to be plumb full of tiny little clay figures, each one obviously handmade by the Leamans. There were figures of people, all with little clothes, figures of animals and of some of the buildings there on the farm.

As Janice carefully unwrapped each one to examine them, she did so with different eyes than she had as a child. She realized that each one of those dozens of figures was carefully made, obviously made with hands as loving as they were skilled.

With a shock, Janice realized that all these figures represented the people, the animals and the buildings and the events of life on the Leaman farm. There was one of a horse pulling a one-bottom plow, faithfully followed by a man on foot, unmistakably Mr. Leaman. There was one of the Leaman girls gleefully swinging in the old tire swing that had hung in the front yard of that place for many years. There were many others.

Tears sprang to Janice's eyes as she held there in her hands some lovingly crafted objects representing the history of the family. She cried as she realized what a beautiful thing that was, and how wonderful it would have been to have been part of doing such a thing for her own family. She cried as she recalled the shallowness of her own youth, as she would so flippantly dismiss such objects as being a bunch of "that Leaman junk." She cried over all the lost opportunities she had had to be a decent person.

Her regrets over how she had so mismanaged her own life came rushing over her to the point that she thought she was going to faint.

Those sobs brought Janice's husband to her side in an attempt to find out what was going on up there in the attic where he could hear that crying.

It was a watershed day for Janice. It was the day she had to pay for the foolishness of her childhood. We are all faced with that, of course, but it was particularly hard on Janice.

Finally recovering from her experience, she carefully rewrapped the little figures, determined to find the Leaman family and return the box to them.

But they were gone. They were gone from the community and couldn't be found. Janice made a number of attempts to locate the family, but came up with nothing.

Upon discovering that she wasn't going to be able to find the rightful owners of all those beautiful little painted figures, Janice decided to use them herself. She decided to equip each of the figures with a little piece of thread and use them to decorate the Christmas trees.

"I thought that doing that might be an opportunity for me to pay my respects at Christmas time each year…….pay my respects to a family that I had grown to admire very, very much. Christmas seemed like a good time for me to celebrate my own growing up. I figured that I grew up a lot that day in that attic as I handled the objects of a family with lots of love and lots of imagination."

Janice's experience up on the floor of that attic that day profoundly affected her husband also. He had known the Leamans and had done his share of teasing them and making fun of them. He had his own need for making amends for the follies of his youth.

Janice did put a tiny thread on each of those little figures, and did use them for Christmas tree ornaments.

"Janice, that's a really nice story, but I thought you had a ghost story for me," I remarked.

She smiled at me and told me it was a ghost story.

"Every year, we put those ornaments on our Christmas tree, and every year it is the same."

She then went on to tell me about how, in the still of the night, those figures would each do their thing. The one of Mr. Leaman would show evidence of having accomplished some of the plowing he was doing. He and his rig would be turned around, plowing in the opposite direction come morning.

Janice and her husband would hear the squeaking of that tire swing each night after going to bed. They would see one of Mrs. Leaman's cookies that would be intact when they went to bed, but find a bite out of it in the morning.

Those Christmas tree ornaments squeaked, mooed, oinked and laughed their way through each Christmas Eve night, with evidence in the morning of how much fun they had. It was the fun of a loving family, each doing their thing and enjoying each other even if they did have snotty neighbors.

Janice went on with another observation.

"Just the other day, I read a very interesting sentence. It was:

>'Travel is not seeing new things as much as it is seeing things with new eyes.'

"I was deeply affected when I read that sentence. It makes a lot of sense, that sentence. And I thought after reading it that our travel through life is a lot like that. It isn't a matter of seeing new things as much as it is seeing things with new eyes."

Even as our interview was coming to an end, Janice found tears welling up in her eyes.

"I believe it was the ghosts of that family that were the cause for those clay figures reliving the lives of the Leaman family. I believe those figures yet, today, somehow embody the ghosts of that family."

The Corpse

It's not too often that a ghost gets into helping to solve a crime. They seem to tend to not concern themselves with doing anything practical. Ghosts seem to be pretty good at walking through walls, clinking chains in the night and going "bump" or "ding" or "scrape" or whatever any one of them is up to.

But apparently a ghost got involved in a very practical situation in Northumberland County in the 1930s.

The situation was the need to solve a crime, and the crime was one of murder. Apparently a fellow had been murdered back then, and a crucial part of solving the crime consisted of the need to find the corpse.

And, finding the corpse proved to be one element of the whole thing that didn't seem like it was going to happen. The law enforcement folks who got involved in the investigation simply came up empty handed.

This whole thing was supposed to have happened in June, and the investigation drug on for months, but still no corpse.

A chief suspect in the case was a farmer who had a place next door to that of the victim.

His place had been gone over with a fine-toothed comb, looking for that corpse, but to no avail.

December brought the first snowfall to the area, and it seemed, at first, to be an ordinary sort of snowfall, one that wasn't any different than any other such snowfall.

A barnstormer was traveling through the area and the pilot noticed the form of what appeared to be a human being down in a field. This fellow didn't know but what the fellow was in deep trouble, lying out in that field, or what was going on. He brought his biplane down low and circled the figure a number of times, but couldn't get a good fix on if the form was really that of a human or if it was dead or alive.

The fellow's solution to the problem was to land in a pasture nearby and walk to the farmhouse so as to call the local authorities about his discovery.

That call alerted the long arm of the law to drive out to the area described to see if someone was, indeed, lying out in a field. Again, the law didn't know if the fellow was a fellow or not, and if he was dead or alive.

52

Arriving to the site described by the pilot of that airplane, the lawman found the figure, just where it had been described.

It proved not to be a person after all. It was simply a portion of the field on which the snow had apparently melted as it fell. While there was an inch or so of snow around that area, the area itself was black dirt. That field had been fall plowed, so all the man got for his effort in trudging out there was a tough quarter mile of working his way out through the mud.

The lawman was about halfway back to his car when it occurred to him that what he had seen was certainly odd. The shape described by that snow free area was remarkably like the shape of a human lying on the ground.

How could that be? It was an open field, with no one part of it any different than any other part. It simply made no sense that a small section should have failed to accumulate snow much like the surrounding area. And, why was that shape so much like that of a human being? The pilot had noticed that, and it was obvious why. It definitely was in the shape of a human, even the right size for an adult human.

The man looked at the sea of muddy field he had had to struggle through to get out to the site and to get halfway back. But, he knew he had no choice. He had to trudge back out there to look at the thing again. So, that is what he did.

Getting back out to the site, the fellow couldn't help but notice that the black soil that showed so well before was still doing so. Even as he watched, he could see the snowflakes accumulating on the snow around the area, and melting as they hit that soil. How in the world could such a thing be?

The man hated to think of having to kneel down in that snow and mud, knowing full well what is was going to do to his nicely cleaned and pressed uniform, but he did.

He scratched some of the mud away, hoping to find a clue as to what was going on by digging down a ways.

He found a clue all right. He found the remains of what was obviously an adult human, and found it right exactly where the image was there several inches above the body.

That unsolved crime of several months earlier came to mind as the fellow quit digging, knowing he'd have to send a crew out to recover the body. He knew he was on the land of the fellow who had been suspected of that murder back in June, and thought he might well have the answer that they had been looking for.

And, he had.

The body proved to be that of the murdered man who had disappeared six months earlier. And his hunch that the previously investigated neighbor was the culprit turned out to be accurate. Confronted with the evidence, the man confessed and that crime was solved.

But, how could that snow have melted so precisely above the remains of the murdered man? The body had been there more than long enough to have lost all its body heat, so that couldn't explain it.

But, the folks there in Northumberland County came up with the answer. Eventually that answer was the one that got to be generally accepted as to what had happened. That answer was that the ghost of the murdered man had caused that snow to melt as it hit the ground that concealed its mortal remains.

There were never further reports of the ghost of that fellow showing up, so apparently all it wanted to do was to lead the law to the perpetrator, and it must have found its rest after that.

The Big Squeeze

Jesse Hopkins wasn't a greenhorn out in the woods by any means. Back in the first decade of the 1900s, most men in rural America were well versed in the practice of woodsmanship. And, like virtually everyone else, Jesse knew his way around cutting trees down, bucking the wood up into firewood and all those skills necessary to turn trees into a nice warm room.

But, things can go wrong, even for the most adept of folks. And so it was for Jesse.

Jesse apparently wasn't after firewood the day he met his maker out there in the woods. He was in the process of cutting a large limb out of a maple tree. He had spotted a hive of wild bees living in that branch, and he wanted to cut it down so he could harvest the honey.

There are few people left anymore who have experienced the heavenly treat of eating wild honey. While tame honey can be really, really good, it cannot begin to compare, in taste, to the wild variety.

Wild honey is gathered from honeycombs that bees will build up in a hollow branch or the trunk of a tree. Just enough of the chemicals of the wood will seep into the honey that it gives it a taste that is dramatically different from the taste of tame honey.

Many years ago, wild honey was plentiful, there being a lot of wild bee trees in the woods. Jesse Hopkins had located such a tree here in Bradford County, and was eager to harvest that bounty of nature's candy.

Jesse's find in that sprawling big old silver maple tree was going to be a lot easier to get to if Jesse could cut out just that one large limb rather than to cut down the entire tree. Back in those days there weren't such things as chainsaws, so cutting down a large tree with either a one-man crosscut or a two-man crosscut was a fair amount of work.

Jesse's decision to cut out only that one large limb was an unfortunate one. It necessitated that he position himself in that group of trunks and limbs such that he would have to be very, very careful that he didn't get pinched between the limb and a nearby trunk. He must have known that when that big old limb started to come down he'd have to leap aside so he wouldn't get pinched. When a couple-thousand-pound limb pinches against a nearby trunk, whatever is in between is going to get squeezed just real good. If that thing between such a limb and such a trunk is a human being, he is going to quite literally have the life squeezed right out of him.

That was the risk that Jesse was running as he was working on getting that limb with the honey in it. Jesse knew enough about the various woods that he knew the nature of the sound that would come from the limb as it started to come down. For each wood, it is a different sound, but Jesse knew 'em all.

No one ever knew, except, perhaps, Jesse. No one ever knew exactly what went wrong that day. We don't know if the limb broke suddenly instead of easing its way down, or maybe Jesse simply didn't move fast enough in getting out of the way.

Whatever happened, Jesse ended up between the end of that limb and the adjacent tree trunk. He was squashed like a bug between those two parts of that cluster of silver maple trees.

It was Jesse's son who was sent to locate his father, and found him dead at the base of that maple tree.

It was a tough day for the Hopkins family just as is a tough go for a family who loses a member today.

That tragedy left the responsibilities of firewood gathering to the eldest son. He picked up where his father left off.

The lad simply couldn't bring himself to harvest any firewood from that silver maple tree, the tree that had been the cause of his father's death.

That grotesque half-fallen tree stood in stark contrast to the otherwise neat woodlot there at the Hopkins' place.

A neighbor noticed that and recognized that the Hopkins' lad was simply avoiding cleaning up that kind of messy residue of his father's honey project. This neighbor talked to the Hopkins son, and offered to come over and clean up that mess himself so the lad wouldn't have to look at it anymore.

That was fine, so the arrangement was made. The neighbor would clean up that old maple tree and could have the firewood for his trouble.

The Hopkins' boy was glad to be shed of that tree and the neighbor could well use the extra firewood.

That would have been the end of the whole thing except that the neighbor found he couldn't use the wood in that tree. Every time he put a piece of it in the fire, he would hear the moans and groans of a man, obviously under intense pain. Apparently the ghost of Jesse Hopkins haunted the wood of the tree where he had died.

The neighbor used that wood only a couple of times before he was able to understand what was going on.

While it was a pretty serious waste of good firewood, the neighbor loaded it all up on a wagon and took it out to a ditch out at the end of the farm where it could rot away in peace.

Somewhere in Bradford County is a ditch filled with what is now only the humus of a maple tree long ago rotted away……a maple tree that served as the home of the ghost of a man who was simply out to get a tub of nature's candy.

The Hand

Any boy who has skinny-dipped in the backwaters of a river very much knows he can be swimming along and find spots in the water that are warmer or colder than the rest of the water.

I'm sure there are people who can explain how that can be. Undoubtedly it has something to do with differential heating, temperature inversions or some such carryings on.

To a boy swimming on a hot summer afternoon, these hot or cold spots are simply unexplainable happenings that can provide a pleasant (or even unpleasant) surprise. Sometimes when it is hot early or late in the summer, a fellow will happen into a particularly warm spot. That feels great! On the other hand, a cold spot one can find in the middle of August can be awfully refreshing. Most of the water will be dull and soup like in feel. Suddenly it's cool and feels cleaner. It's a good feeling.

The two Ellis boys and their buddy, Dean Kane, were taking a dip in the Susquehanna. It was one of those doggy days of

August. One of the guys had thought he knew where to find some of those patches of mid-summer mushrooms. Finding any mushrooms that late in the year was a novelty so the boys had looked long and hard. It was all in vain. They were hot and tired so decided to go for a swim to cool off.

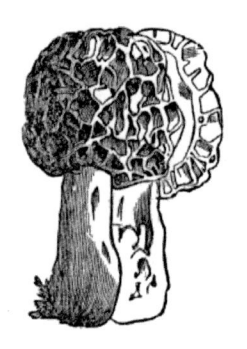

As the boys were swimming toward a patch of lily pads, it was Dean who first noticed a strange thing. Apparently he was out ahead and so got into it first. It was one of those cold spots. This one was different though......much different. It wasn't a matter of a few degrees different. The water didn't change from tepid to only warmish, or even down to cool. The water suddenly became very, very cold. Instantly the boys started to shiver.

The fellows tried to talk to each other, to say something about what was happening, but they couldn't. Their teeth were chattering with the cold and their now blue lips would hardly move.

It was Dean who was telling me the story of what happened there over a half-century ago now.

"I was really scared. I'd never seen such a thing before. I'd spent a lot of time skinny-dippin' the river, but never saw anything at all like that before. I don't ever want to go through that again, either. I was shivering so much I couldn't holler out when I saw that hand floating by Jeff's shoulder. Jeff was five or six feet away from me, and there was that hand!"

"A hand?" I asked.

"Yep. It looked like a man's hand, kind of rough like, you know. I tried to tell Jeff about it but couldn't. Jes' about then Jeff saw it, too. So did his brother. We all three saw that thing."

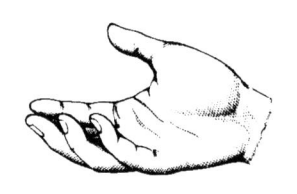

"So, what happened then?" I asked.

"Well, Jeff was jus' a more than tearing up the water there trying to get away from that hand. He was really thrashin' around. If he had taken his time, he could easily have swam away, but he was trying too hard.

"With all that splashin' around, the hand disappeared. Sank, I guess. Just then the water went back to feeling normal again. That coldness just seemed to flow away from us. Just being normal made it feel hot compared to what it had been for ten or fifteen seconds just before then."

I asked Dean if the hand floated back up to the top again after it quit splashing around.

"Nope, never saw it again. Believe me, we got out of there. In fact, we quit swimming for the day."

A story about a floating hand in the river isn't exactly a ghost story. A chilly spot doesn't make a ghost story either, but maybe the two together is too much for a coincidence.

Perhaps the cold spot is a ghost or associated with a ghost. Perhaps the ghost was following the hand down the river. We have no idea what was going on that hot day in August back in '53, but whatever it was, those three boys never forgot it.

Gold From The River

Sally and Lee Sand never did manage to accumulate very much of this world's possessions. It wasn't any single thing that could count for that. They didn't suffer from chronic bad luck or go through any dramatic financial reversals. They just never seemed to be able to set a few dollars aside.

Part of the problem was that both Sally and Lee would give whatever they had to whoever needed a hand. The reservoir of poor is always full, of course. This was especially so down along the Susquehanna during the '30s. The Sand's cabin there north of Wilkes-Barre was a refuge for every kind of down-and-outer for a quick meal or a bed for the night.

What little that Lee made fishing and Sally with her housework for the local rich ladies didn't go far with such a crying need around them all the time.

In the spring and summer of their lives, Lee and Sally didn't think much about what their needs would be as they would grow older. As that time approached, however, they began to realize that they were in trouble.

Fortunately, the Sands had one stroke of very good luck. While fishing, Lee pulled into his boat a wooden barrel drifting by. This large barrel apparently fell from a boat or something.

The barrel was full of personal belongings such as clothes and such. The bulk of it, however, consisted of several very old and valuable gold coins.

Sally and Lee had a day better than several Christmases in a row when they found all the goodies in that barrel.

"It sure was lucky there was enough straw in the barrel to keep it floatin'. If'n it'd bin any heavier, it woulda' bin setting on the bottom 'stead of floatin' down the river!" exclaimed Lee.

The Sands kept that gold in their shack for only a few days before Sally found a buyer among the ladies she did housework for. The lady came to the cabin and was quite impressed with the beautiful pieces and so agreed to buy them all.

The arrangement involved the delivery of the gold to a dock downstream from the cabin where the buyer's husband was to pick it up there where he could park his car.

As often happens, good luck often draws bad luck. In this case, it was more than bad. It was tragic. Apparently Lee suffered a heart attack, for he collapsed and died somewhere between leaving the cabin and getting to that dock where he was to deliver the gold.

It could have been a double tragic loss for Sally. The boat could well have continued to drift on downstream. She might have lost their newly found fortune in addition to her husband.

Something, however, caused that boat to drift back upstream. Several people on the shore saw it happen. The boat returned to the cabin, contrary to all logic and explanation. Sally was able to retrieve the gold coins, and did sell them to the fancy lady.

The proceeds of that sale allowed Sally to live the rest of her life with a measure of comfort and security.

How did that boat drift upstream? How could that happen with no one rowing it? Legend has it that the ghost of Lee Sand somehow got that boat going back up against the current to return that treasure to Sally.

Perhaps a freak current or eddy along the shore caused it to drift back to the cabin. Perhaps there is some other explanation of that strange event.

For my part, I prefer to believe the old legend that it was Lee's ghost doing one last generous act to see to the well being of his lifelong partner.

A Bubble Off

The Nason family had long lived in that house at Berwick that had been in the family ever since the middle 1800s.

There were reminders of specific individuals in the house and on the grounds……individuals from out of the family's past.

One interesting such reminder was the limestone windowsill in the shed that Grandfather Silas Nason was alleged to have lifted into place with bare hands. Weighing in at probably over four hundred pounds, that windowsill represented a rather impressive feat.

But, more interesting than that were the "scientific" papers that would turn up in the darndest places. These papers were exercises in scientific thought, and were the products of the somewhat disjointed Great-Uncle William.

Apparently Great-Uncle William was a self-taught individual. Perhaps the words self-deluded would be more appropriate since these papers certainly reflected the musings of a person who was undoubtedly a bubble off of plumb.

The family had a long history of finding these papers. Early on, in the twentieth century, they showed up in logical places, such as in the attic or squirreled away in a box in the basement.

Through the years, enough of these "scientific" papers had been found that it was pretty much assumed that the family had found 'em all.

And, they saved them. They were not only products of a colorful family member, but were humorous in their content.

Some of the memorable ones were On Interplanetary Travel Via Mental Efforts and On Potential Means of Adapting Auditory Organs to Gills for Submarine Respiration.

That latter one was the favorite among several members of the family. Apparently Great-Uncle William was hot on the trail of figuring out how to turn ears into gills so we could breathe under water.

Another favorite was Probability as a Function of Gastric Digestive Processes. While that was one of the favorites in the family, no one could quite figure out how Great-Uncle William had cooked up some relationship between mathematics and digestion.

Others of those papers were so obscure that no one could figure them out. A couple such were <u>Peptide Molecular Structure and Lunar Dislocations</u> and <u>Posthumous Ocular Transfer Capabilities as Related to Ocular Particulates</u>.

The meaning of those last two were simply beyond any in the family. But, they got kept just like all the others the family had found.

It didn't take long for the family to develop the tradition of breaking out all those old papers whenever they'd get together for holidays. They would get all kinds of fun out of trying to figure out what that was all about.

Great-Uncle William had handwritten all those papers. Bad as his handwriting was, folks could generally figure out the words in the titles, but couldn't begin to decipher the smaller and more scrawled out text of the papers.

But, the titles alone provided folks with lots of amusement at holiday get-togethers.

Things got a bit mystifying when they found one of those papers down within an attic wall, dated 1914. The fact that it was dated wasn't cause for concern. What confused the family was that date since Great-Uncle William died in 1905.

Part of the fun of talking about those papers was speculation that Great-Uncle William was still working on his scientific experiments after his death.

There was speculation that he was probably still working on that stuff way up there in the attic. There were those in the family who guessed that the old man might still figure out how to turn ears into gills.

None of that was taken seriously since it was generally agreed that the date 1914 on that one paper should have been 1904, and that the old duffer had simply misprinted it.

Everyone knew that the old man was long gone and there wasn't a ghostly lab anywhere in the house.

They should have thought that one over a bit.

It was in 1985 when one of the family members developed some vision problems..........problems sufficient to cause the doctor to recommend retiring to a darkened room for several days.

So he did.

But that didn't do the job. After the prescribed period of time, his vision continued to be out of whack.

By that time, his visual problems had been reduced to one single problem. It was the darndest problem Brad Williams, the victim, had ever encountered.

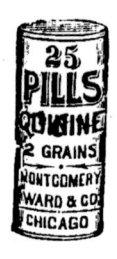

Brad had long experienced having "floaters" in his eyes. We all do. Floaters are those temporary and ill-defined transparent images that occur to one when he is looking at a featureless thing like a blank wall.

They generally kind of float around in one's field of vision. We are so accustomed to them that we don't usually even see them.

The thing about Brad's floaters is that they became much larger in size than what had been normal. These things are usually very small circles or fibrous-shaped things that occupy a very small portion of one's field of vision.

It was another trip back to the doctor to figure out a way to solve that problem.

Since these floaters are actually microscopic dust particles or air bubbles, the doctor provided Brad with some drops to use to rinse his eyes out a couple times a day.

It was obvious to the doctor that Brad needed to practice some enhanced eye hygiene and the problem would be solved.

But, there was another problem that Brad didn't share with the doctor. In fact, he hadn't even told his wife about it. He was afraid that he would not be believed, and even ridiculed for imagining things.

Since those images had grown in size, they occupied a significant portion of his field of vision. It was what he saw when he looked through those little images that disturbed Brad to no end.

He'd see things that were different than when viewed through the non-floater portion of his field of vision. He saw any object as it would have looked earlier in time when he viewed it through one of his enlarged floaters.

He first noticed it when he happened to look out toward an old pine tree in his yard. When viewed through one of the floaters in his eye, it had the appearance of a sapling. When viewed outside of that floater, out in the regular field of vision, it looked like it was…………..an old, old tree.

Brad looked out across a neighboring cornfield, and that's what it looked like in his normal field of vision. But through the floater, it turned out to be a grove of trees. It was as he was looking into the past when he looked through one of those things in his eye.

Brad was bothered to no end about this, but didn't breathe a word about it. He didn't want to be thought to be a bubble off.

After all, you don't look into the past by any means, eye trouble or not.

The eye drops didn't do a bit of good. It got worse. The sizes of those floaters got greater. It got to the point that Brad was seeing more of how things used to be than he was seeing things the way they actually were.

Brad had gotten to the end of his rope, and was desperate to find a solution. That is when he told his wife what was going on.

Rita was far less concerned about who thought who was a bubble or two off. She herded him back to the doctor and insisted that he spill the whole story to the doctor.

Guess what? The doctor suggested some psychological counseling. That was, of course, exactly what Brad had feared and foresaw.

But he went along with it, and had a couple visits with a shrink.

It wasn't helping. By now Brad would look out across the room and see more old-fashioned overstuffed chairs and antique appointments than he would see the things as they really were. He found it necessary to maneuver a person he was talking to into the little remaining portion of his field of vision that reflected reality in order to carry on a conversation.

Rita and Brad shared the situation with the rest of the family, explaining that Brad's eyes had degenerated to the point that he was seeing far more of the past than he was the present.

It was at one of those family get-togethers when they did this. That festive practice of going over those old scientific papers of Great-Uncle William was replaced by a discussion of the situation and what could be done about it.

They had about come to the conclusion that nothing could be done about it.

Brad's dilemma was that there was no way he could share with others what he was seeing. He tried to explain it, but one can't see out of another's eyes. He wanted his family to understand that what he was going through was real and it wasn't all in his head.

He despaired about the possibility of doing that, and was almost resigned to the fact that people would be thinking that it was all in his head.

One of the couple's sons was a physics major at the university, and was particularly interested in his father's problem. His scientific bend led him to try to understand the problem more than the others.

Suddenly this young man, Robert, sat bolt upright in his chair and wanted to see those old papers of Great-Uncle William.

His mother tried to ignore that. She didn't think it was appropriate for the family to be amusing itself in reading those old papers. But Robert insisted.

The lad turned to those few totally indecipherable papers in the back of the stack and found what he was looking for. It was a paper entitled <u>Posthumous Ocular Transfer Capabilities as Related to Ocular Particulates</u>.

Robert's eyes narrowed as he studied that title, then widened in disbelief.

Others in the family wanted to know what his surprise at that paper was all about.

Robert was silent for a few minutes, then proceeded to share some thoughts with them.

He pointed out that his study at the university had led him down a lot of paths. These included his using words generally used only by practicing scientists. His work at the university had led him to an understanding of some of those big words that had previously only been big words.

"Let me put the title of this paper of Great-Uncle William's into everyday English.

"It really reads…the transferring of sight to a deceased person by means of the floaters in the eyes of another person.

"This paper is about how to see through someone else's eyes after you die, to see by means of using visual floaters."

The ticking of the clock and the snoring of the dog over by the sofa were the only sounds heard in that room with a number of people in it.

Robert was telling them that that goofy old paper of Great-Uncle William's was telling about the possibility of seeing through someone else's eyes.

That, of course, struck a chord immediately with everyone in the room.

That old duffer had written a paper about the very thing that was obviously affecting Brad.

"Robert, are you telling me that the old man was studying something that would be the very reason for my problem?"

"I sure am, Dad. Never would I have thought that that old duffer was on to something that he could really bring about. And, remember how we found that paper that was dated several years after the old man died?

I hate to the be the first one to say it, but maybe the ghost of Great-Uncle William is still working away in his lab somewhere here in the house? And it looks like his idea of transferring vision to the dead works."

Again, a silence that seemed to last forever. Then everybody wanted to talk at once. The concept of Great-Uncle William still doing his thing in that house was an idea that sparked all kinds of reactions.

"Be quiet. I'll handle this."

Those words from Rita silenced the whole crowd. Rita still had tears in her eyes, tears that came so easily anymore………tears that spoke of the frustrations of seeing her husband degenerate either mentally or visually. She wasn't sure, herself, if he had slipped into irrationality or not.

"I'll handle this. Robert, you and your dad come with me."

With that Rita rose and started up the stairs to the second floor.

Not knowing what else to do, the two men did just that. Robert had to help his dad because all Brad could see anymore was a confusing mix of what was real and what was out of the past.

The three of them went up to the second floor of the house, then on up into the attic where the bulk of those papers had been found, and where the one that Robert had singled out had been found.

The two men had no more of an idea of why they were there than they did when they got up from their chairs in the living room.

Rita sort of straightened an errant strand of hair and launched into her reason for being there.

"Great-Uncle William, I am here to make a deal with you. I believe you are still among us in one way or the other. I believe you are still doing your research and it appears that you are onto something with your work on transferring vision from the living to the dead.

"You have chosen my husband to act as your vehicle to vision here on this earth. He is paying dearly for this, as am I."

Brad and Robert were both stunned at this turn of events. They sure hadn't expected to be party of a lecture to a ghost, but that was exactly what Rita was doing.

"It occurs to me that we have done you an injustice by making fun of your papers. We have been callous enough to gain entertainment at your expense. I am sorry for that, and apologize for what we did. I promise you that it will never happen again.

"I'm here to make a deal with you. If you take this vision problem from us, we will leave you to do your work in peace. We will never enter the attic again, except to do repair work if and as that is necessary.

"If you fail to correct the problem my husband is suffering from, then I promise you from the bottom of my heart that I will burn this house down to the ground. I will prevent any efforts to put the fire out. I will deprive you of your laboratory. I will do this in a heartbeat without so much as a backward glance."

With that, Rita turned, motioned for the two men to follow, and went back down the stairway.

Both Brad and his son were so stunned by what had happened in the past few moments that they could hardly talk.

Back down in the living room, Rita announced to the rest of the family what she had done, and that was the way it was going to be.

It was a sober and contrite bunch that went to bed that night. Her mother was openly determined to burn the house that had been in the family for many generations. There was surprising little talk about that little lecture that Rita had delivered up there in the attic.

It was in the morning that the talk about the whole situation filled the house, as each person had an opinion about the whole thing.

Never had the family expected their mother to do such a thing.

And then there was the second reason for lots and lots of talk. Brad woke up with his vision perfectly restored. If he concentrated on it real hard and looked at a blank wall or an open window at the sky, he could detect a floater or two in his eyes, as can any of us.

But they were all but invisible, and much smaller than they had grown to be just a few hours earlier.

So, where does all this take us? Was the old man really just a befuddled old codger who was a bubble off? Did he really figure all that out about how to see through someone else's eyes? Was that the work of his ghost, and is that ghost still doing his thing in that old house in Berwick? How much reality is in what we see, and how much reality is there in things unseen?

Those are all good questions yet today.

Paintin' The Coop

You'd sure think that a couple could go for a lifetime without arguing over something as dumb as what color to paint a chicken coop. Fact is, most couples can do just that. Bill and Edie Blencoe from around Liverpool couldn't quite make it. Their henhouse needed a coat of paint so Bill set out to do it.

The daughter who told me the story didn't know how the argument all got started, but once it got going there seemed to be no stopping it. He wanted white and she wanted it to be a light blue to match the house. Seems the issue got so hot that it held up the painting job 'til folks could cool off.

The daughter told me she felt neither of the pair really cared that much one way or the other, but once they had committed themselves to a color, it was easier for both of them to insist on having their way than it was to cave into the other.

The whole thing started to come to a head again when it was looking like the job could actually be done. He kept saying the only logical color was white and "whoever heard of a blue chicken coop, anyway?"

"Mama's attitude was that she didn't give a fig what most people did. She wanted blue, and that was that!"

"We kids, meanwhile, were making bets among ourselves as to who would win."

"Why, I remember, I and my younger sister had a bet. If Dad won, I was going to do the dishes alone for a full week. If Mama won, my little sister was going to do them for that week. Neither one of us were the least bit interested in doin' dishes, so each of us was rootin' for our side."

"What did your folks think of you two betting on the outcome of their argument?" I asked.

"I don't know. We didn't tell 'em about it. I guess we figured that they both would have whomped us good if they knew."

It was with a bit of a giggle that this now gray-haired daughter told of how both her parents had pretty good tempers and how her mother pitched a frying pan at her father one day over the issue.

"Well, who finally won?" I asked.

"That's where the ghost part comes in. Mama died that March. She never had been in good health after Bernice was born. I was really too young to know much of what was goin' on, but I did know she was poorly. Anyway, we lost Mama in early March of 1924. I was only eight years old at the time, but I remember her very well.

"After Mama died, a lot of things were different. My older sister took care of us littler kids, and Dad eventually married a lady from over at Newport. By the time they got married, we kids were just about grown up. But I'm gettin' ahead of my story. Dad painted that chicken coop along about May or so. He painted it white, jus' like he had bin arguin' for."

"So, where does the ghost come in?" I asked.

"I'm sure it was Mama's ghost that came back right after Dad painted the coop. Dad finished up that paintin' job early in the evening. Come mornin', he looked out of the window to see how his work looked in full daylight. What he saw was a light blue henhouse. That color jus' plain changed color in the middle of the night. It changed to the same color Mama wanted all the time. When he went out to see it, he took the two oldest boys with him. He asked my brothers what color the henhouse was. They agreed that it was light blue. Dad bought white paint and he put white paint on that building. The little bit 'a paint that was left in the can was white and that he had spilled on the ground was white. But that old henhouse was blue, the exact blue Mama wanted. She had kept pointin' to a dress in the mail order catalog and telling Dad that was the color she wanted. We compared the color to that dress. Exact same color, it was."

"So what did your father do about it?"

"He left it blue. He said that he had done all the arguin' about it he wanted, and he sure wasn't goin' to argue with a ghost about it.

"Fact is, it got to be a sort of family tradition. Every time after that when Dad painted the coop, it was light blue.

"My brother, Leo, took over the farm in the 1940s, and he kept the coop blue. His boy, today yet, keeps the chicken coop blue. It's a different coop now. The old one rotted down, but the new one is in the same place and is still blue. Both Leo and his boy had to get special mixed paint to get the right color, but that's what they did. The fella down at the hardware store told them one day that it was kind of silly to special mix a paint for an old chicken coop, but then that fella did not know the story about how it all got started."

"Maybe after that fellow reads this book, he will know," I suggested.

"I don't much care one way or the other about that guy. It'd be nice, though, if Mama were to know that Dad and Leo and Leo's boy all kept the coop blue after that."

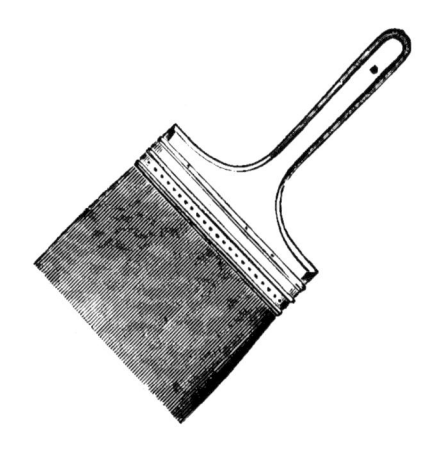

The Flower Girl

Lucas Brenner liked to sit on the porch of his cabin on a summer evening there near Williamsport. The moonlight would be reflected off the water, giving the appearance of a huge white walkway out across the river.

It wasn't that anything ever happened out there of any particular interest. Oh, sometimes he would see some critters come into view and then disappear again. It was just restful to sit there on that porch and watch the water shimmer out in that wide band of reflected moonlight.

Lucas was doing just that one July night in 1948. He had spent a long day fishing. When he had gotten all done, he had cleaned the cabin out. Lucas liked to tidy up a bit every few weeks whether the place needed it or not.

He had finished his work and was sitting out that porch with a long, tall glass of iced tea.

When he first saw that girl out on the water, he felt he must have dozed off and dreamt it. After all, how many times can a person look out on the water and see a gal strolling around on it like it was an ordinary sidewalk?

The more Lucas blinked his eyes and pinched himself to be sure he was awake, the more convinced he became that he really was awake, and what he saw simply wasn't his imagination.

She was two or three hundred feet away, but he could see that she was a beautiful girl. She was carrying what appeared to be some flowers and had the air about her that she wasn't really going anywhere, just out for a walk. On occasion, her movement was more akin to a dance than a walk.

The girl came over to the bank. In fact, she came up on the bank a few feet before walking on out again onto that wide strip of light on the water's surface.

By this time, Lucas was halfway down to the water's edge as he tried to keep the girl in his sight. He lost her, though, as she walked out of that moonlight into the darkness.

Lucas returned to the cabin porch and waited almost an hour for the girl to come back, but she never did. He knew by now that he was fully awake. He still couldn't understand, of course, how that girl could have done that, where she came from or where she went.

Lucas stayed up a couple of hours later that night, looking out over the river on occasion to see if he could see that beautiful apparition strolling around again. His watch was in vain. He never saw her after that first time.

Come morning, the first thing Lucas did was to prop himself up in his bed to look out of the window onto the river, remembering the events of the night before. There was nothing out there much different than what he'd seen every morning for many years. The water was there, the trees still stood along the bank and the water lilies still lay in the nearby cove where he kept his boat. There sure wasn't any beautiful young lady walking around out on the surface of that water that morning. He hadn't really expected to see her, but he was still disappointed.

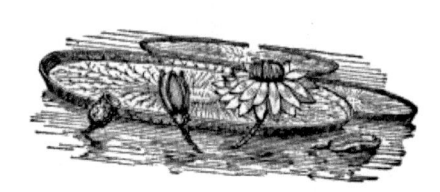

Lucas slipped on his clothes to go down to check a throw line before he got things started for the day. All his line yielded, however, were two small bullheads that he pitched back into the water.

Just as he had thrown that line back out and turned to go back to the cabin is when he saw something different on the bank. At first it was just a flash of color he saw out of the corner of his eye. What he found there was a nice fresh rose dropped in the mud along the bank. It looked like it had just been dropped. It hadn't been washed up by the water. That blossom had never been in the water.

Lucas looked at that rose a long time without picking it up. How could it have gotten there? It sure hadn't been there the previous evening when he set out that throw line. No one was likely to have been at that spot through the night. He remembered, then, the flowers carried by the girl who walked on the water.

Carefully Lucas reached for the flower. As he picked it up, it looked like any ordinary rose. That is, it looked quite ordinary for a few seconds.

Then, without warning, that blossom turned dry and brown right there in his hands. Lucas dropped that flower like he'd been stung. Standing there, shocked, Lucas watched the fragments of that flower drift lazily out into the river.

So who was the girl in the moonlight? It's not everybody who can walk around out on the top of the water. Lucas was convinced she must have been a ghost of some kind.

Why she carried the flowers or why one of them she previously dropped should turn to dust as Lucas picked it up is a mystery.

Lucas never saw the girl again.

The Tap On The Shoulder

Pickford Jones was an arrogant, opinionated, pig-headed man. You've probably known someone like him – always thinks he has the answer to every question, doesn't take kindly to being interrupted or contradicted. And, the thing that makes people like Pick hardest to swallow is the fact that they are often right.

Pick never went to school beyond the eighth grade, but he did a tremendous lot of reading about everything from cattle breeding and the internal combustion engine to St. Augustine and the Great Wall of China. And he was more than happy to explain anything he knew to anyone who'd listen, as long as they didn't contradict or interrupt. They may not have always loved him, but folks couldn't help but respect him for his mind and his business savvy.

He loved automobiles and got into the business of selling Chryslers to the people around Lancaster in the 1920s. He also sold some used ones of earlier vintage. As long as it was a car, he'd deal in it.

You might say that Pick and the automobile grew up together. He drove his first car when he was too small to look over the dashboard. And he liked to drive. He also liked the insides of a car, its engine, transmission and all its mechanical systems. He could hold forth for hours on this component or that, and was likely to ask questions like "Do you know which part of the automobile has never changed since the first ones were built?"

And when you didn't know the answer, he'd get a kick out of telling you.

In the winter of 1934-35, one of the local undertakers came into Pick's showroom.

"What have you got for a hearse?" he wanted to know.

Well, of course, Pick didn't have any in stock, but he got his order books and they put together a deal.

When the hearse came in, Pick was very proud of it and showed it off to the undertaker like the car salesman he was. He always did have the flair for the dramatic.

"And," Pick said, "I'll drive it for you the next time you need it."

That was fine with the undertaker. He wouldn't mind some company the next time he went to pick up a body in the middle of the night.

It was a few days later that the call came in. Old Mr. Weingarten had died in his bed and Mrs. Weingarten would like the undertaker to come and pick him up.

Yes, she was sorry it was so late, but really, could he please come right away.

The undertaker called Pick and asked if he'd like to come along.

"Of course I will. I'll be ready by the time you get here to the house."

The Weingarten farm was on down toward Mountville, so it wasn't too long a drive.

When they started for the Weingartens, it was foggy. Pick was driving and he couldn't see much more than a few hundred yards.

"You're sure you don't mind helping me with the body?" the undertaker wanted to know. "Some folks are kind of squeamish about bodies."

Pick was very sure, as usual.

"It's only a body and I don't believe in all those superstitions."

The undertaker and Pick went into the Weingartens home and carried Mr. Weingarten out.

While they loaded him into the back of the hearse, Pick kept commenting about what a fine hearse the undertaker had. He pointed out how nice the doors worked and how convenient everything was. The undertaker just nodded. He was used to Pick going on like that.

While Pick was raving about the gasoline capacity, the engine sputtered and died. Fortunately, Pick knew the fellow who owned the farm just down the road, and he went to see if he could roust him out and borrow a can of gas.

While the undertaker waited in the hearse, a scruffy-looking man came up alongside his door and asked if he could hitch a ride.

The undertaker was surprised a hitchhiker would want to ride in a hearse, but the guy said there hadn't been any other traffic through there in a couple of hours and he needed to get back to town.

The undertaker told him he could come along, but he'd have to ride in the back and he wanted him to understand they were hauling a body.

When Pick came back, the undertaker opened his mouth to tell him about the hitchhiker, but Pick launched into a speech about something or other, and never gave him a chance.

On a night like that, you can start talking about all kinds of strange things. There were swirly patches of fog, and it was drizzling. What with a body in back and driving a hearse, Pick got off on one of his favorite topics – superstition. He allowed that he didn't believe in any of it, that a dead body was nothing but a dead body. The soul was long gone, and it was only a shell.

The undertaker agreed with him privately, but he saw a chance to goad Pick a little, so he asked him what he thought of a certain story he'd heard about a haunted house around there.

Pick got up on his soapbox and spent at least ten minutes repeating that there were no such things as ghosts, haunted houses or any of that mumbo-jumbo.

Finally Pick stopped for breath, and the undertaker started to tell him one of his favorite funeral home stories.

Pick had heard that story before and stopped him in the middle of a sentence.

"That doesn't prove anything. I'll tell you again, sir, that everything can be explained in logical terms."

That was when Pick felt a tap on his shoulder. He swerved the hearse nearly off the road. He just about got it straightened out again when a voice behind him asked a question.

"Hey, mister, you got a light?"

The undertaker nearly went through the windshield when Pick hit those brakes. Pick didn't wait for the hearse to stop. He was out that door and gone, hightailing it into the fog before the undertaker could get his balance and grab the steering wheel.

The next day the undertaker saw Pick at a Rotary lunch and thought he looked a bit peaked. He couldn't resist asking him if he'd had a nice walk, but he never could bring himself to tell Pick about the hitchhiker.

Down The Stairs

Tim and Iris Fantell had an interesting ghost in their home in Duncannon. This was undoubtedly the ghost of Old Man Harrison, who had lived in that house back a full hundred years before the Fantells did in the 1990s.

Way back then in the 1890s, when Old Man Harrison lived there, the old fellow had a pretty awful day in the summer of 1897.

Apparently Old Man Harrison was in pretty good shape for a real old duffer. The fellow bragged about being born on the very day of the death of George Washington, so that put him right at 98 years old in that summer of 1897. While the old fellow was said to be in pretty good shape, he did find it necessary, back then, to get around the house with the aid of a good stout hickory cane.

It was while he was up in the attic heading for the top of the stairwell when the fates caught up with the 98 year old. The floor up in the attic was one of those old-fashioned yellow pine board floors.

Usually a knot will stick tight as a tick in a yellow pine floorboard, but Old Man Harrison's luck ran out that summer day back in 1897.

The knot in that board right near the top of the stairs had probably hung in the knothole for lots of years when Old Man Harrison's cane landed right smack on that knot. When the old man put a little weight on his cane, the knot let go. It slipped right out of the knothole, allowing the cane to drop down and pitch the old man forward.

Unfortunately, of course, since he was approaching the top of the stairs, getting pitched forward popped the old fellow right down the stairs, head over heels.

You don't go around pitching 98-year-old men down attic stairways without doing a whole lot of damage to all kinds of body parts.

Old Man Harrison was apparently still with us when he ended up lying on the floor of the second floor, but that didn't last long. By the time a family member got upstairs to him after his fall down those stairs and got him loaded up in a vehicle, it was all over.

After all the excitement and turmoil of the day, the family found the old man's cane, still stuck in that knothole at the top of the stairs. They didn't even bring the cane downstairs. They simply stuck it in a corner by the dormer window up there in the attic. A dead man wouldn't have a whole lot of use for a cane, of course.

Maybe sticking that cane in a corner up there was a mistake. It was still up there a couple generations later when the Fantells moved into that house in the 1970s.

Maybe if that cane hadn't been up there, the Fantells wouldn't have had their ghost problem.

It wasn't a matter of wondering what this ghost was going to do next. Theirs was a very predictable ghost.

It all started out with the couple hearing the steps up there in the attic. It'd always be the same, the shuffling steps of an old person accompanied by the periodic stomp of the end of a cane……..a heavy old cane.

Then, when the sound of those shuffling footsteps approached the top of the stairwell, the Fantells would hear the pop of a knot cutting loose from its knothole. This would be followed by a stumbling thud, then the sound of a frail old body catapulting down the stairwell.

The Fantells would rush up to the second floor to be greeted only by the door from the hallway up to the attic being open. There would be no sign of anyone up there, least of all the body of an old man born on the day of the death of George Washington.

After a while, both of the Fantells knew what to do next. They'd go up to the top of the stairway and find that old cane stuck away in its corner, just as it had been for decades. Each time this would happen, however, they'd find the dust on the handle of that cane wiped clean.

The couple would shut the door at the bottom of the stairs and wait for the next shuffle-pop-tumble-thud episode.

A couple of times through the years, the Fantells toyed with the idea of getting rid of the cane, and perhaps getting rid of their ghost.

They decided, however, that they'd rather have a very predictable ghost who confined himself to the attic and an occasionally quick trip down to the second floor…………..over one who might take to wandering about the house. So they left the cane there for the old fellow's convenience.

The Odd Case Of Dimples Darmhoff

"Dimples" wasn't her real name. In fact, the writer of this story doesn't even know her real name. Dimples Darmhoff had been known by that name for so many decades that many, even in her extended family, didn't know her real name. She was either Dimples, Aunt Dimples, Great-Aunt Dimples or Grandma Dimples.

Dimples and her husband, Arron Darmhoff, lived in the old home place outside of Bloomsburg in the 1970s and '80s, well after the last of their children had grown up and left.

But everybody being grown and gone didn't keep Grandma Dimples and Grandpa Arron's place from being the gathering point for family get-togethers.

And, it was during these get-togethers when Arron would spin a tale for the benefit of the little kids.

It was always the same story………the same corny story, but the little kids loved it. The big kids would roll their eyes around and pretend to be bored with the whole thing……..even as they'd jockey for positions near their grandfather as he would tell that story.

Grandpa Arron would tell the children about when he fell in love with a dimple when he was a young buck. He'd go on and on about that dimple, and how hard he fell in love with it.

He'd tell about how he proposed marriage to that dimple. And, that was how he ended up being married to its owner.

The old man would explain to the children that he didn't really have any ambitions to marry the children's grandmother. It's just that since the dimple was hers, he had to take her along in the deal.

As Grandpa told that story, the little kids would stand around the old man's chair, wide eyed and dry mouthed.

They would hear all about how their grandfather had fallen in love and married a dimple.

The grandfathers of most children simply married those children's grandmother, but not those kids. Their grandfather married a dimple……can you imagine that?………..married to a dimple!

Arron had lost an arm as a child, but put the remaining one to effective use as he'd gyrate around flailing that remaining arm to emphasize this or that point in his tale of his odd romance.

Dimples would join in with the older kids in rolling her eyes around in impatience, but Grandpa didn't care. At this point in the process, he'd be so engrossed in his story that nothing would even slow him down.

It was a good story, made even better by the little children's firm belief in that line.

Arron's snow-white beard and that deep voice made for effective points of emphasis, besides his flailing his one arm around as he did.

Had they been asked, those little kids in that large family would have guessed that life would go on that way forever. Grandpa's stories, Grandma's dimple that would form at even the slightest smile or feelings of pleasure, Great-Aunt Betty's unbelievably good peach pie and that long sledding hill were simply parts of life that had always been and would always be.

One of the blessings of youth is the delusion that such circumstances never will end. But all those things, except for the sliding hill, eventually disappeared.

It started with the death of Grandma Dimples in 1988 when she went on to that giant family get-together in the sky.

Apparently Grandma Dimples' funeral was, like many funerals, one that didn't quite come off without a minor hitch or two.

The particular detail that went wrong at that funeral was that the family had neglected to provide the funeral home with Grandma's skinny little gold wire-rimmed glasses.

Grandma Dimples wouldn't be Grandma Dimples without those glasses, of course. So, on the morning of the funeral when those glasses were found there at the house, one of her sons simply announced that he'd take those glasses with him to the funeral and slip them onto his mother's face while she laid there up by the altar in the front of the church.

It was that little situation that resulted in this story ending up in this book.

Eric, the son, was going to be very coy and slip those glasses onto his mother's face before the funeral got a good start so she'd have them on when folks came to pay their last respects.

Eric had given those glasses a good washing off there at the house before leaving for the funeral. After all, it wouldn't do to have anything but nice shiny glasses on Grandma Dimples for the occasion.

As Eric stood there at the side of that open casket, he couldn't help but relive all the many memories from his childhood as he gazed into the still face of his departed mother.

He recalled how a wisp of hair always seemed to be out of place, and how she was always tucking that behind her ear.

As he stood there he couldn't help but notice how she didn't look quite natural without her glasses on. And the funeral director had not caught that dimple that would spring so readily to his mother's face at the slightest hint of pleasure.

Eric thought about how a good report card, or a good job of washing behind his ears as a child, would bring that dimple to life so quickly. He recalled about how a torn shirt or his teasing the cat would erase that dimple in a heartbeat.

The dimple was gone now, and Eric knew he'd never see it again……..not in this life, anyway.

Eric slipped the glasses out of his breast pocket and gave them a final "look through" to be sure they were good and clean and hadn't picked up any lint from his pocket.

It was that quick glance through the lens of those glasses that resulted in a series of events that was never to be forgotten by the family members that were at that funeral.

What was going to be simply a quick glance turned into an intense study of those glasses.

Eric didn't see the expanse of red carpet there at the front of the church………that red carpet that had been there for so many years.

In the place of that carpet was the old yellow pine floorboards that had been covered up by that carpet many years earlier. The casket carrier wheels were resting on those old yellow pine boards instead of that red carpeting.

Confused, Eric lowered the glasses to where he could see that carpeting again.

Putting them back up close to his eyes, he could see, once again, that old-fashioned wooden floor he recalled from his childhood.

Unable to fathom what was going on, he turned out toward the pews of the church.

The crowd of friends and relatives was gone, replaced with the lone figure of a young man……..a one-armed young man.

While this young fellow's features were familiar to Eric, he saw no evidence of the white beard that should have been part of that countenance.

Eric recognized the suit the young man wore. It was the suit he had seen pictures of………pictures of the wedding of his parents. It was a wedding that had taken place at that exact spot in that same church way back in the late 1920s.

As was shown in that old, old photo, the left arm of that suit coat was tucked neatly in the pocket of the suit's jacket. That's how his father had done it on those rare occasions when he'd be wearing a suit.

It was at that point that Eric realized he was watching an image of his father as he was waiting for his marriage ceremony to get started….his marriage to a dimple. It was a dimple that happened to come with a whole person; a person he got along with the dimple he had fallen in love with.

It was the shocked look on Eric's face that led his wife to come up the couple of steps to see what was ailing her husband.

Eric's coy little plan to slip those glasses onto the face of his mother had gone seriously awry. He was standing there, apparently almost in total shock, moving those glasses up by his eyes, then lowering them again, looking through them, then over them, in an effort to understand what was going on.

Wordlessly Eric handed those glasses to his wife. Not knowing what else to do, she looked through them and saw things in that church that had existed long before she had even been born.

She saw the bell rope hanging down through the ceiling, a rope that hadn't seen the light of day for decades. She saw those yellow pine floorboards and the benches that had long since been replaced by manufactured pews. She, too, saw a young man she recognized to be a much, much younger version of her father-in-law.

Wanda exhaled a long breath, having forgotten to breathe as she had found herself observing circumstances as they had been many decades earlier.

Wanda's surprised gasp drew the attention of others in that crowd of people there in the church……..people who were quite visible when viewed without those glasses, but people who all disappeared when the scene was viewed through the glasses.

A couple of them came up to Eric and Wanda, fully aware that something was way out of whack with that couple.

Others viewed the interior of the church that day through those glasses. All agreed with each other as to what they saw. They were obviously getting a view of the day that Grandpa Arron and Grandma Dimples got married.

Somehow, Grandma Dimples or her ghost had engineered things so that the images of that day of sixty years earlier came to life again when one wore those glasses. If this was Grandma Dimples' ghost at work, how and why would she do that?

How could time be erased simply by donning a pair of glasses? Was Grandpa Arron, sitting out there in his wedding suit, really there? Was that a strange reality that sprang into existence as a result of putting those glasses on?

It was obvious to all that they had, in their possession, the strangest pair of glasses in all the world. It seemed to be a pair of glasses that could turn back the hands of time.

A whispered conversation among the small knot of relatives there by the casket led them to make a decision. It was decided that they would go ahead and bury those glasses with Grandma Dimples.

So, while watched by a bunch of tear-stained eyes, Eric slipped those glasses onto his mother's face, right past the wisp of hair that always seemed to be out of place.

Without exception, every one of those people saw a change come over the face of Grandma Dimples. A slight smile appeared and her famous dimple showed up once again. It was that dimple that Grandpa Arron had married………a dimple that came with a whole person attached.

So, in a little church cemetery near Bloomsburg is a pair of glasses adorning the remains of a lady who, somehow, had imparted a property to those glasses that enabled them to erase many years of time. They erased enough time to bring back the day of her marriage to a young man with an empty sleeve, a sleeve neatly tucked into his suit coat.

The Inconvenience

When Ben and Alice bought that old brick house, they neither knew nor cared about the history of the place. All they knew was that the price was right, and it would make one heck of a nice B&B.

It was a fixer-upper without a doubt, and would involve a lot of work to bring it up to a quality appropriate for a B&B. Still, they thought it was the opportunity of a lifetime.

So, this couple bought the old Victorian mansion, and started down the long road of repairing it and restoring its 1800's beauty.

Ok, I'm lying about this being appropriate for this book. The circumstances detailed in this story didn't happen near here at all. This story really comes to us from London, Kentucky, on I-75.

But, I'm putting this story in this book anyway because it's such a good one. What I'm depending on is that the reader won't read this little bitty print in this footnote...or if he does, that he'll forgive my transgression in putting this story in this book.

Thanks for your indulgence.

In order to save money, the couple decided to live in the place while they were doing the refurbishing. During the course of their work, they found out a bit of the history of the place as they would visit with the neighbors.

The fact that it had been a house of ill repute back in the 1800s didn't really make any difference to them. After almost a hundred years of the house having been a private residence, neither Ben nor Alice expected anyone to confuse their new place with a house of ill repute.

The work progressed slowly as it always does when you are trying to bootstrap a project.

And, of course, there were any number of times that problems arose that gave them second thoughts about the wisdom of doing the project.

It was Ben who was most easily discouraged by the setbacks they would encounter.

Alice, on the other hand, was more inclined to take the long view, and to realize that when they got done with it, it would be a beautiful place, well worth the time and money to make it all happen.

During each of those times that Ben would question if they should continue, Alice would counter with her standard answer... "It'll all work out alright."

Ben could just about depend on hearing that...

"It'll all work out alright" whenever he'd suggest they sell the place, and move on.

Then, one night, an event took place that changed everything. It was after a hard day's work that Ben had gone to bed early. He was bushed, and all he wanted to do was hit the sack and get some sleep.

He had just crawled into bed, fluffed his pillow up to his liking and closed his eyes.

Suddenly, as he laid there on his side ready to go to sleep, he felt someone get into bed with him. This sort of surprised Ben because Alice had, just a few minutes earlier, told him that she was going to stay up and put one more coat of varnish on some woodwork they were working on.

Besides that, Alice had a habit of getting into bed as if she were mad at it. Ben had often told her that she got into bed like a 70 pound keg of nails.

His bedmate there sure didn't get into bed that way. It was a matter of kind of gently sliding into bed.

As Ben laid there, about to question Alice why she decided to come to bed after all, the second surprise came along. That surprise was in the form of a warm and gentle puff of breath on the back of his neck.

Now, Ben had been married long enough to know that Alice gently easing into bed, and giving him a provocative puff on his neck was totally out of character for her.

He turned to face her, and found a..........nothing, nothing at all. He had the bed all to himself, no wife, and no warm breath on the back of his neck.

Ben marveled at how he could be dreaming such a thing, not two minutes after laying down. He decided that he was even more tired than he thought, and had gotten to sleep as soon as he got that pillow squared away.

Ben went on to sleep with no further ado.

And, the project of fixing that house up continued. Ben was convinced that it was a never-ending job, and they'd be staining woodwork and hanging wallpaper when they were old and grey. But, he never did come up with a rebuttal to "It'll all work out alright."

It was about two weeks later, and Ben went to bed early again. He wasn't dead tired this time like the last time he had crawled in the sack alone, but just thought he'd get to bed early, and get up early.

The same routine...the laying on his side and the punching around on the pillow until it felt just right.

This time Ben hadn't yet even closed his eyes, and again there was that gentle sliding into bed next to him, followed by a provocative warm breath on the back of his neck.

Wow, this was just like that dream he had a couple weeks earlier, except this time he was awake. Ben wondered why Alice had suddenly taken up behavior that was so out of character for her.

"What's with your sliding into bed that way, Honey? What happened to your hitting the sack like you're mad at it?"

No answer.

"Honey, what's with your sneaking into bed that way?"

Again, no answer.

Twice he had talked to her, and she hadn't answered either time, so he turned so he could see her.............No Alice.........no anybody.

This time Ben knew he had something on his hands other than simply dreaming. Something was going on that needed explanation.

Ben laid there a moment, studying the pillow next to him when the thought struck him that this might be the work of a ghost. Alice was alive and well, he could hear her rattling the dishes out in the kitchen as she cleaned up after their supper. It couldn't be Alice's ghost 'cause she wouldn't have one.

It was at that moment that he put two and two together and came up with the theory that his bedmate, temporary as she was, was the ghost of one of those fallen doves who had inhabited the house almost a hundred years earlier.

Now, good lookin' honeys softly sliding into bed with a fellow and puffing warm breath on his neck is something of a cause for celebration, even if she is a ghost.

Ben contemplated the situation as he laid there, about as wide awake as one person could be. He came to the conclusion that this house was a good idea, even if it was a lot of work and expense.

Sometimes there are intangible rewards in taking on a project, don't you know.

So, it was off to sleep for Ben, thinking of this good looking raven-haired beauty that had crawled into bed with him. Okay, so he made up the raven-haired part, but sometimes you have to improvise, you know.

Ben developed a new concern. He was concerned about the possibility that his experience that resulted from him going to bed early was not going to be repeated. He need not have feared that. From that point on, that happened a number of times.

Ben didn't bother Alice with all that. She had a lot on her mind, and he didn't want to unduly concern her. Ben was very considerate that way.

But, he chose to tell his buddies about his ghostly visitor. Actually, it was more of a case of bragging to his buddies about that.

Alice noticed that her husband had fewer bouts of wishing they hadn't gotten started on the B&B project. She was glad he was finally coming to see that things will all work out alright.

You know how things are. A buddy will tell his wife things, then his wife will talk to Alice and next thing you know, Alice knows all about the warm-breathed Honey.

It took some tall talking on Ben's part of explaining all that. He put it in the context of a dream, and how he only dreamed all that stuff, and he was really getting tired of having that same old tired dream every once in a while.

Ben took the precaution of holding his hand behind his back and crossing his fingers. He recalled that was a sure fire way of making it perfectly OK to cancel out the moral problem of telling a lie. He remembered that from his childhood. Everybody knew it was OK to lie if you crossed your fingers while doing so.

Surprisingly enough, Alice bought that. Perhaps she had been sniffing too many varnish fumes and didn't realize that Ben was lying through his teeth. They weren't dreams at all, much less dreams that Ben had tired of.

So, Alice put all that behind her. Besides that, you can't blame a fellow for having bad dreams, even if they are dreams about a ghost of a red-headed Honey. Ben had no idea where the "red headed" part came from, but figured that one of his buddies got the story wrong.

In spite of Alice's steadfast nature, the problems of redoing a large old Victorian house started to wear thin for her. So, when they discovered a leak in the roof that would require some expensive repair work, she wondered if they ought to give it up.

"You know, Ben, maybe what we ought to do is sell this place. You've been saying that for a long time now, and I think that maybe you're right."

Oops, this was a development that Ben wasn't ready for, much less come up with an argument against. He knew it was going to take some fancy footwork on his part to jump over to the other side of this "leave" or "not leave" issue.

"Yeah, well, we need to think about that, of course."

It was the best response Ben could come up with since he didn't have time there at the kitchen table to do the fancy footwork he needed to in order to switch sides on that issue.

"After all, Ben, when folks are paying a good price to stay in our B&B, they sure aren't going to appreciate what feels like a little honey crawling in bed with them and puffing warm breath on the back of their necks."

"Oh, no, of course not," Ben replied, hoping that he sounded half way sincere.

Having what seemed like Ben's agreement, Alice went on about how guys sure wouldn't want that inconvenience after a day's driving behind them, and another day's driving ahead of them.

Ben couldn't help but to think to himself..."What an inconvenience! What an inconvenience!"

This story took an unexpected turn as Ben was telling it to me.

"So, did Alice ever catch on to you?"

I had learned earlier from Ben that Alice had passed away shortly after the two of them finished up their B&B project. So, I wondered if she had learned about their ghost before she died.

"No," Ben said, "She never learned the truth, but there is sort of a sequel to this whole story."

"What's that?" I asked.

"Well, it wasn't long after Alice left us that those visits took on a new twist. The new twist was that if I'd go to be early, on occasion, I'd feel someone get into bed beside me, but after I lost Alice, it wasn't a matter of sliding into bed. It was still a ghost 'cause she'd be gone when I turned over."

"How, then, was it different?" I asked.

"It was different because after I lost Alice, my bed partner would get into bed like a 70 pound keg of nails........just like she was mad at the bed."

My Own Ghost Hunting Notes

My Own Ghost Hunting Notes

My Own Ghost Hunting Notes

My Own Ghost Hunting Notes

My Own Ghost Hunting Notes

My Own Ghost Hunting Notes

My Own Ghost Hunting Notes

My Own Ghost Hunting Notes

GHOSTS OF INTERSTATE 90 Chicago to Boston   by D. Latham

GHOSTS of the Whitewater Valley by Chuck Grimes

GHOSTS of Interstate 74   by B. Carlson

GHOSTS of the Ohio Lakeshore Counties   by Karen Waltemire

GHOSTS of Interstate 65   by Joanna Foreman

GHOSTS of Interstate 25 by Bruce Carlson

GHOSTS of the Smoky Mountains by Larry Hillhouse

GHOSTS of the Illinois Canal System by David Youngquist

GHOSTS of the Niagara River   by Bruce Carlson

Ghosts of Little Bavaria   by Kishe Wallace

Shown above (at 85% of actual size) are the spines of other Quixote Press books of ghost stories. These are available at the retailer from whom this book was procured, or from our office at 1-800-571-2665 cost is $9.95 + $3.50 S/H.

Ghosts of Interstate 75	by Bruce Carlson
Ghosts of Lake Michigan	by Ophelia Julien
Ghosts of I-10	by C. J. Mouser
GHOSTS OF INTERSTATE 55	by Bruce Carlson
Ghosts of US - 13, Wisconsin Dells to Superior	by Bruce Carlson
Ghosts of I-80	David youngquist
Ghosts of Interstate 95	by Bruce Carlson
Ghosts of US 550	by Richard DeVore
Ghosts of Erie Canal	by Tony Gerst
Ghosts of the Ohio River	by Bruce Carlson
Ghosts of Warren County	by Various Writers
Ghosts of I-71 Louisville, KY to Cleveland, OH	by Bruce Carlson

GHOSTS of Lookout Mountain by Larry Hillhouse	
GHOSTS of Interstate 77 by Bruce Carlson	
GHOSTS of Interstate 94 by B. Carlson	
GHOSTS of MICHIGAN'S U. P. by Chris Shanley-Dillman	
GHOSTS of the FOX RIVER VALLEY by D. Latham	
GHOSTS ALONG J-35 by *B. Carlson*	
Ghostly Tales of Lake Huron **by Roger H. Meyer**	
Ghost Stories by Kids, for Kids by some really great fifth graders	
Ghosts of Door County Wisconsin by Geri Rider	
Ghosts of the Ozarks *B Carlson*	
Ghosts of US - 63 by Bruce Carlson	
Ghostly Tales of Lake Erie by Jo Lela Pope Kimber	

GHOSTS OF DALLAS COUNTY	by Lori Pielak
Ghosts of US - 66 from Chicgo to Oklahoma	By McCarty & Wilson
Ghosts of the Appalachian Trail	by Dr. Tirstan Perry
Ghosts of I-70	by B. Carlson
Ghosts of the Thousand Islands	by Larry Hillhouse
Ghosts of US - 23 in Michigan	by B. Carlson
Ghosts of Lake Superior	by Enid Cleaves
GHOSTS OF THE IOWA GREAT LAKES	by Bruce Carlson
Ghosts of the Amana Colonies	by Lori Erickson
Ghosts of Lee County, Iowa	by Bruce Carlson
The Best of the Mississippi River Ghosts	by Bruce Carlson
Ghosts of Polk County Iowa	by Tom Welch

Ghosts of Ohio's Lake Erie shores & Islands Vacationland by B. Carlson
Ghosts of Des Moines County   by Bruce Carlson
Ghosts of the Wabash River   by Bruce Carlson
Ghosts of Michigan's US 127   by Bruce Carlson
GHOSTS OF I-79   ***BY BRUCE CARLSON***
Ghosts of US-66 from Ft. Smith to Flagstaff   by Connie Wilson
Ghosts of US 6 in Pennslyvania   **by Bruce Carlson**
Ghosts of the Lower Missouri   by Marcia Schwartz
Ghosts of the Tennessee River in Tennessee   by Bruce Carlson
Ghosts of the Tennessee River in Alabama
Ghosts of Michigan's US 12 by R. Rademacher & B. Carlson
Ghosts of the Upper Savannah River from Augusta to Lake Hartwell   by Bruce Carlson
Mysteries of the Lake of the Ozarks   Hean & Sugar Hardin

To Order Copies

Please send me _____ copies of *Ghosts of Pennsylvania's Susquehanna River* at $9.95 each plus $3.50 for the first one and $1.50 for each additional copy for S/H. (Make checks payable to **QUIXOTE PRESS**.)

Name _____

Street _____

City _____ State _____ Zip _____

QUIXOTE PRESS
3544 Blakslee Street
Wever, IA 52658
1-800-571-2665

To Order Copies

Please send me _____ copies of *Ghosts of Pennsylvania's Susquehanna River* at $9.95 each plus $3.50 for the first one and $1.50 for each additional copy for S/H. (Make checks payable to **QUIXOTE PRESS**.)

Name _____

Street _____

City _____ State _____ Zip _____

QUIXOTE PRESS
3544 Blakslee Street
Wever, IA 52658
1-800-571-2665